THE SHOWDOWN

BERNARD PALMER

Tyndale House
Publishers, Inc.
Wheaton, Illinois

Bernard Palmer is also the well-known author of the Breck Western Series and My Son, My Son. *He lives with his wife, Marjorie, in Holdrege, Nebraska.*

The Danny Orlis Adventure Series
The Final Touchdown
The Last Minute Miracle
The Race Against Time
The Showdown
The Case of the Talking Rocks
The Sacred Ruins

Previously published by Moody Press under the title
Danny Orlis Star Back.

First Tyndale House printing, February 1989
Library of Congress Catalog Card Number 88-51655
ISBN 0-8423-0557-2
© 1957 by Bernard Palmer
Printed in the United States of America

Contents

ONE
An offer hard to refuse

Danny Orlis went out of the little log house where he
lived with his father and mother and the twins. He
walked down to Pine Creek, which shimmered like a
mirror in the early morning sun. He stood an inch taller than his dad's six feet this summer and weighed a
sinewy 185 pounds. Rowing and swimming every day
all summer did it. Chopping wood, cleaning out under-
brush, working in the garden accounted for arms and
legs muscled with steel. He could work alongside of
any man on the Angle.

Danny stopped momentarily and looked around.
The little packet boat, "Valiant", lay motionless at the
dock, and the "Scappoose" was pulled up in front of
the guest cabins and securely tied. Bill Martin and
Cap were still asleep in their sleeping bags in the
prow of their boat; the fishermen in the cabins were
just beginning to stir.

Danny sat down cross-legged on the end of the dock.
His dog, Laddie, padded stiffly up to him. He patted
the big dog tenderly on his shaggy head. The faithful

old fellow was getting old and lame with rheumatism. He could scarcely get around. Laddie turned and looked up at him, his big, soft eyes as sad as though he knew his master would soon be going away.

"Yes, sir, Laddie," Danny said. "It's going to be lonesome down in Cedarton this winter."

"It's going to be lonesome around here, too, Danny," a voice said behind him.

He turned quickly to see his young adopted brother, Ronnie, standing barefooted on the rough planks. "Hi, Ron, I didn't know you were up so early."

Ronnie squatted beside him on the dock. "I wish you weren't going to have to go away to school this winter."

"I know, but that's the way it's got to be. In another year you and Roxie will be in the ninth grade. Then you'll have to go away to school, too."

"I know," the younger boy told him. "I wish I didn't have to leave the Angle, though. I wish I'd never have to leave."

"That's the way I feel about it up here, too," Danny went on. "It's hard to leave home and go away to school." His dog stretched out beside him comfortably and rested his nose against his knee. "It's hard to keep a strong testimony for Christ when you're away from the folks. Especially when most of your schoolmates aren't Christians."

"The kids don't ra z you or anything, do they, Danny?" Ron asked uncertainly. "Because you stand up for Christ, I mean?"

"Sometimes they'll give a guy an awfully rough time," Danny admitted. "But they'll admire you and respect you if you stand firm for what you know is right."

A big mallard wheeled by overhead, and they both watched until he winged his way across the narrow creek and dipped down behind the trees.

"I don't know whether I could do it or not, Danny," Ron went on presently. "That's the thing that worries me."

For a couple of minutes the older boy did not answer. "You won't be able to if you depend on yourself, Ron. You've got to put your whole trust in Christ, keep in close touch with him, read your Bible and pray every day. If you do that and refuse to compromise—if you take a strong stand for the Lord on the very first day and don't give an inch from it, you'll be all right."

"You make it sound easy."

"As long as you're depending on the Lord Jesus and not yourself, it is easy."

Ron moved over and took Laddie affectionately by the ear. "When are you going down to Cedarton, Danny?"

"I don't know for sure. Got a letter from Rick Haines yesterday. He said the guys are starting football practice the Monday before school starts, and I don't want to miss that."

Just then one of the fishermen stuck his head out of the cabin door and called to Danny. "Hey, fella, come here a minute."

"Sure thing," Danny replied, jumping to his feet. "I'll be right there."

"I'll see you in the house," Ron said softly. "I think Mother must have breakfast ready by now."

"Would you have your mother pack a lunch for us?" The fisherman asked Danny when he reached their cabin. "We want to be gone all day."

"OK," he replied. "Will you want me to guide you?"

The fisherman shook his head. "Nope," he said. "We can find our way."

Something about the way the man spoke bothered Danny vaguely as he went up to the house to help his mother make sandwiches and coffee for them. But he soon got busy with other things and forgot about it. There was always so much to do the last days before going away to school. He had new rabbit hutches to help Ron build, some more wood to saw and pile for winter, and a small stack of hay to put up for their one cow. Then there was the new trap line Ron had asked him to help lay out.

"It was a good thing those guys didn't want me to guide them," he said aloud, "or I'd never get all this done."

"I was thinking the same thing myself," his dad replied. "I've been wanting to go in to town and take care of some business before you leave." He looked up at the gathering clouds. "I was planning to fly in to town with Tex if he gets here before the storm."

Tex flew in just before dinner, ate hurriedly with them, and he and Mr. Orlis took off for Warroad.

"That storm is coming up fast, Danny," Carl Orlis called as he crawled into the little float plane. "If those fishermen aren't back here in half an hour or so, you'd better go out and look for them."

"Which direction did they go?"

"I don't know for sure," Mr. Orlis replied, "but they were asking me about Harrison Creek last night. You might take a look up that way."

"OK," Danny said.

He went back into the house while the plane took

off, and got his raincoat and jacket. The wind was kicking up choppy waves and the clouds were gathering just above the trees. It would not be long until the bay would be rolling whitecaps and the rain would be sweeping across the muskeg. He would have to find those fishermen fast.

"Want to go with me, Ron?" he called.

The younger boy grabbed a piece of cake from the table and came out, stuffing it into his mouth.

"Better get your coat," Danny said. "I'll fill the 'Scappoose' with gas."

Finally Danny Orlis started the powerful old motor on the "Scappoose" and headed out of the mouth of Pine Creek into the wind-tossed bay. They went out into the lake and angled into the teeth of the wind. He took a quick look at the clouds that were churning ominously overhead. In another twenty minutes the storm would hit.

"I hope those guys have sense enough to get into one of the creeks and stay there until this blows over," he said more to himself than to Ron. "That's one thing you want to be sure to do, Ron. If you get caught out here in a storm, get to the closest shore; get up into one of the creeks if you can."

The "Scappoose" lifted and fell sluggishly with each long, rolling swell. Danny took a quick, anxious look along the shoreline and cut the speed of the laboring boat. Speed would only drive her prow deeper into the waves, causing her to wallow sluggishly.

The wind came up even higher. A few drops of rain went skittering across the waves.

"Here it comes, Ron!" Danny's younger brother hunched his back against the storm.

Danny inched the boat closer to the shore and had Ron put on one of the life jackets in the prow of the "Scappoose". If those fishermen were experienced at all they would not have to be worrying about them. The bay was long and could get so rough nobody would want to be out on it, but it was narrow too, and there was no reason a boat could not get ashore safely. But you could not tell what a greenhorn would do, especially if he got scared.

Danny squinted into the driving rain. Just as he had suspected, the fishermen were in trouble, their boat was floundering helplessly in the middle of the bay. The motor had stopped and both men were working with it, unmindful of the storm. The little craft had swung about until it lay lengthwise in the trough of the waves. Water silled into it from every whitecap and it rolled dangerously.

"Boy, we're just in time!"

He held his breath as the boat pitched.

"We've got to get out there, quick!" Ron exclaimed.

The older Orlis boy opened the throttle. The "Scappoose" thrust her prow into the air and began to knife into the waves, sending the spray flying. When they neared the other boat, Danny cut his speed.

"Use your oars," he shouted to the men above the roar of the storm. "Swing her around until she's riding with the waves!"

"We don't have any oars! Forgot to bring them!"

"Oh, boy!" Ron exclaimed. "What are we going to do?"

"Loosen the anchor rope," Danny ordered. "Take the anchor off and toss the rope to me."

Danny tied one end of the rope to the carrying

handle at the back of the "Scappoose", coiled it, and angled toward the floundering craft.

"Sit down!" he shouted to the men in the boat who stood when they saw what he was about to do. "Sit down! I'll get the rope over to you!"

He brought the "Scappoose" expertly about and moved toward the tossing boat. When he was within half a length of it he tossed the rope to the man in the prow.

"Tie it to the seat," he ordered.

Danny Orlis slowed the "Scappoose" to a crawl as the rope tightened and the helpless boat began to come about. It was a long, slow job to carefully tow the other boat in the storm, but they finally reached the mouth of Pine Creek and turned in.

"We were certainly glad to see you," one of the men said when they were in the Orlis home and in dry clothes.

"I was glad to see you, too," Danny answered. "I didn't have any idea where you were." He straightened a little. "There's one thing I've been wondering, though. What were you doing with that rifle in the boat? I saw it out there a couple of minutes ago."

The men looked at one another queerly.

"Well," the self-appointed spokesman said, "I guess there's no point in lying. We thought we'd go out and see if we could get a deer."

Danny's face clouded.

"But we didn't see any," the fellow hastened to add.

"It's a good thing," Danny told him. "Dad has never allowed any of our guests to break the game laws. You would probably have found yourself on the way to Kenora or Warroad to the game warden, depending on which side of the line you made your kill."

"We got cold feet anyhow," he said. "We'd never have killed a deer. But Bill and I were just talking on the way in. If you'll guide us every day, we'll stay until after Labor Day."

Danny looked quickly at his mother and Ron. He knew how badly his folks needed the money, but that would mean missing the preseason football practice. And with the good players Cedarton has this season, they could beat him out of a place on the team!

TWO
Tough competition

"Danny can't do that," Ron put in. "He's got to get down to Cedarton in time to go out for football. They start practicing next Monday morning."

"There'll be time enough to go out for football after school starts," Danny said. "I'll be glad to stay and guide you."

"That's fine. We've had enough of going out in that lake alone."

When the Orlis boys were outside later, Ron turned to Danny. "Why did you tell those guys that you would stay and guide them? If you don't get down to Cedarton to start practice when the other guys do, they'll have all the positions sewed up. Then what will you do?"

"The folks need all the money they can get, Ron, and I need all I can make guiding, too. I've got a lot of school clothes to buy."

"I suppose you're right. But I sure hope you make that team. You've got to make it this year."

The next few days when Danny Orlis was not out on

the lake with the fishermen, he and Ron passed the football around. They went out in back to a level spot in front of the post office and took turns centering the ball and receiving it, just to get the feel of it again.

On one occasion Danny was practicing those long flat passes Coach Collins liked so well when one of the fishermen happened by and stood watching.

"Say, Danny," he said. "You throw a nice pass. I've been watching you this week."

Danny thanked him.

The fisherman looked him over carefully. "You've got the build for it and you handle yourself like a football player. I'd like to see you run." He got an arm-load of wood from the woodpile and scattered the pieces, ten or fifteen feet apart, across the grass. "Now," he continued, "everyone of those chunks of wood is a tackler. Let's see you dodge them."

Danny felt a little silly pretending that his back yard was full of football players, but the fisherman seemed serious enough. He tucked the ball snugly in his arms and with a sudden burst of speed scampered through the make-believe tacklers, dodging this way and that.

The fisherman walked slowly over to where he was standing. "Not bad, Danny. Not bad at all. It would take a lot of work, but I believe you've got real possibilities as a university player with your speed and size. Where did you say you were going to school this year? I'm going to have one of our men take a look at you in a regular game this fall." He handed Danny his card. "I'm Glen Moore, athletic director of West Farmington. I think we may have something attractive to offer a fellow like you, if you can play as well as I think you can.

Danny's head was swimming as Mr. Moore went back to his cabin.

"Did you hear that, Ron?" he asked excitedly. "Mr. Moore is athletic director of West Farmington U. They play against all the big teams: Minnesota, Wisconsin, Oklahoma, and all the rest. And he says I might be good enough to play with them; just think of that! He was even talking about giving me something just to go there to play football!"

Ron's eyes opened wide. "Oh, boy! You're going to do it, aren't you, Danny?"

Danny stopped a moment. "I don't know," he said. "I don't even have a real chance yet."

"Maybe if you got to play there and did real well you'd get to play with the Chicago Bears or the Cleveland Browns or people like that," Ron continued. "Then you'll make some real money when you get out of college."

"I haven't even made the team at Cedarton yet," Danny laughed. "And here you've got me playing with professionals."

Nevertheless, as he went back to work, Danny couldn't keep his mind off Mr. Moore and what he had said. It all depended upon how well he played for Cedarton that fall. That was a goal to work for.

"We're leaving this afternoon, Danny," Mr. Moore announced on Labor Day morning. "But I want you to remember what I said. Give it everything you've got this fall. We'll be getting in touch with you when the season is over."

The fishermen left the Northwest Angle that afternoon for their home, and early the next morning Tex flew Danny down to Cedarton. He had written for the same room he had occupied the year before in the Barbers' home.

"It's certainly good to be back, Mrs. Barber," he said as he stopped for a moment in the living room before taking his suitcase upstairs.

"It's good to have you back," she answered smiling. "Only I'm not Mrs. Barber anymore, Danny. Mr. Meyer and I were married in July."

"Say now, that's great."

"It certainly is," Wilbur Meyer said as he came into the living room. "I lost Ken last spring, but God not only gave me a sweet wife, he gave me Karen and Kirk as well. Now I have both a son and a daughter."

Danny got his things unpacked as quickly as he could and called Kay Milburn. She had come to Cedarton three or four days before.

"I just got in," he told her. "When can we get together?"

"I've got to go downtown," she said. "Why don't we meet at the ice cream shop?"

Kay had grown taller and prettier in the three months since he had seen her last. Her clear, white skin had become browned by the hot Mexican sun, and her blond hair had lightened. Somehow she seemed so much more mature than she had last May.

"It's good to see you again, Kay," he began as they sat down to drink malts. "Did you have a good summer?"

"Wonderful! You should see the change that is coming over our people since we got the New Testament translated into their language so they can read and study it. The superintendent of the Mission says that more progress is being made in our tribe now than they've ever been able to make before."

"You came a little early this year, didn't you?" Danny asked her.

"I wanted to have time to look around the Bible institute here in Cedarton," she said. "I want to decide where I'm going to school next year so I can get my application in."

"Bible institute?" Danny echoed. "Are you going to a school like that?"

"I think every young Christian ought to go to a Bible institute or Bible college for a year or two first, to get a real grounding in the Word of God."

"But those schools aren't accredited," Danny told her. "It's just a waste of time."

"Some are accredited now so that you could go to a regular university afterward and count the work you'd done toward a degree," she said, "and it isn't a waste of time to study God's Word. A good Bible institute will give you such an understanding of the Bible that you won't be in so much danger of having some disbelieving teacher shake your faith."

Danny was silent. He couldn't help thinking of Mr. Moore and the opportunity to play football for West Farmington U. A Christian football player in a place like that could be a real testimony for Christ. He could have an influence on his companions. And yet what Kay had said was vaguely disturbing. Was he well enough grounded in the Scriptures so that he could stand up against the teaching of an occasional atheistic instructor? Did he know enough about the Bible to be able to hold fast against the teaching of evolution? Could he go to a school like West Farmington U with the assurance that his faith would not become wobbly under the onslaught of doubt and disbelief? And would the influence of his testimony be destroyed?

Kay went on to ask what he had been doing that summer, and how the twins and his folks were. Soon those other questions were pushed, unanswered, into the recesses of his mind.

"We've got a lot to do at school this year," she said as they got up to leave.

"You can say that again. We've got to get some younger kids interested in the Bible club and get them trained so they can carry it on next year."

"You know, that's just what I've been thinking. It would be tragic to see our Bible club die."

Rick Haines was waiting for Danny at the Meyers' home when he got back there just before supper, and told him all about the prospects for the football team.

"We're going to have a powerhouse this year, Danny," the tall athlete said. "We've got the best bunch of football players we've ever had. If Coach Collins can just get us to pull together."

The next day after school when Danny reported for football he saw what Rick meant. There must have been fifty guys out, and it seemed that at least half of them were determined to make the starting eleven.

"What position have you been thinking about, Danny?" the coach asked as he was putting on his shoes.

"I played quarterback my sophomore year at Iron Mountain, Colorado," Danny said.

The coach frowned thoughtfully. "Everybody on the squad wants to be a quarterback this year."

Danny looked up quickly. "It doesn't matter what position I play, if I can just get a chance to get out there."

Out on the field they went through a long series of calisthenics. Then Coach Collins called off the names of those for the A team in a scrimmage.

"The rest of you will be on the B squad," he announced. "Now get in there and show us how much football you know."

Danny sat down on the bench with the B squad while the teams lined up for the kickoff. He had never played football for Coach Collins. If he could just get in there and show what he could do!

The B team kicked off and one of the A's back fieldmen took the ball deep in his own territory. He hesitated a moment while his blocking gathered ahead of him, and then he took off! He headed up field, running like a frightened deer. The blockers took out three tacklers. He dodged a fourth, and shook a fifth loose with a terrific change of pace that sent the would be tackler sprawling. When the ball was downed he had made a run of fifty-three yards.

"Did you see that, Danny?" the boy beside him on the bench exclaimed. "Did you see that run?"

"Who was it?" In spite of himself a little twinge of jealousy gripped him.

"That's Tim Barton," Bruce replied. "Just moved here from Duluth. He was All-State quarterback for two years. Boy, we can sure use him!"

Danny nodded. But, there went his chance of playing quarterback!

THREE
Hit from behind!

Tim Barton ran roughshod over the B team until Coach Collins took him out. He was a smart, fast quarterback with an uncanny knack of spotting the opposing line's weak spots. He could pass like a bullet; he was good. There was no doubt about that.

People who were passing stopped to watch him until there was quite a knot of spectators. Finally Coach Collins blew his whistle and sent in a substitute for the flashy quarterback.

"That's enough for now, Barton," he called. "Stevens," he said to the boy going in, "try that new series of plays we've been working on."

Tim Barton swaggered off the field and stood in front of the B team bench. He was a powerfully built guy with shoulders like a blacksmith's.

"If I'd had a decent line ahead of me," he boasted, but soft enough so that the coach could not hear him, "I'd have made a couple more touchdowns easily." He looked around deliberately to see that he had everyone's attention. "But I guess the line's not so bad at that," he went on, "for a dump like Cedarton. Now up at Duluth I had some *real* football players in the line ahead of me."

"Boy," Bruce whispered to Danny, "he doesn't think much of himself, does he?"

Danny got into the practice just before Coach Collins called it to a halt. However, he got to run off half a dozen plays which made two first downs against the regulars.

"You're doing all right, Danny," the coach told him when the scrimmage was over. "I'm going to use you with the A team tomorrow."

He grinned happily.

Rick waited for him in the locker room until he took a shower and got dressed.

"It seemed good to get hold of the football again," Danny said as they walked home together.

"You did a good job today, Danny. And you didn't get to practice with us last week either."

"I know. But I won't have a chance of getting in the starting lineup. Barton has the quarterback spot sewed up tight."

"He's good, all right. His passes come at you like a rifle bullet, but they're easy to catch. And how he can run! I believe he could beat any sprinter we've got in school."

Danny Orlis nodded.

That night the first Bible club meeting of the season was held at Marilyn Forester's and Danny and Kay went a little early to help with the program. It was a warm September evening and the front door to the beautiful, new Forester home was open.

"It's all right this time, Marilyn," Mrs. Forester was

saying loudly as Danny and Kay stepped up onto the porch. "You've invited your friends so I won't say anything to embarrass them. But don't ask them again. Do you understand?"

Danny looked at Kay uncertainly and stepped back off the porch.

"But why, Mother?" Marilyn asked. "They're such good kids."

"What would my friends think," her mother went on caustically, "if they should happen to drive by the house and hear a lot of hymn singing? I would never be able to live it down."

"Come on, Kay," Danny said, touching her arm. "We'd better walk around the block. We don't want Marilyn to know that we've heard what her mother had to say."

"Poor Marilyn," Kay said, more to herself than to Danny. "It's hard enough to have a strong Christian testimony when you have help from home. It must be terrible for those who don't!"

Danny nodded in agreement. "We want to remember her in prayer. She needs all the help she can get."

"We want to pray for her mother too. She must be terribly unhappy living only for her card parties and club meetings."

When Danny and Kay went back to the Forester home after walking around the block, Mrs. Forester came to the door and greeted them warmly.

"We're so glad to have Marilyn's friends in," she told them, smiling. "Our home is open to you anytime."

There was a big crowd for the first meeting of the Bible club. The group filled chairs, both divans in the long living room, and spilled over onto the floor. The meeting was very informal. Instead of preparing a Bible lesson, the leader called on half a dozen Christian young people for their testimonies, and three or four for their favorite Bible verses.

When the meeting was over Danny turned to see Mr. Forester standing behind him, his hands thrust into his pockets.

"I'd like to say a word before you get out of here," he said to the leader. "This is the first meeting like this I have ever seen, but I just wanted to tell you that I think you've got something. Keep it up. Don't let anyone stop you." He paused. "I wish there had been something like this in Cedarton when I was going to high school. Perhaps things would have been different." He turned slowly in the silence that followed, and walked back into the kitchen.

"Well!" Danny heard Mrs. Forester snort. "I never thought I'd hear anything like that from you!" The the kitchen door closed.

The meeting was over, then, and the kids began to file out. Marilyn came over and took hold of Kay's hand and squeezed it.

"How have you been, Marilyn?" Kay asked her.

"Not so good," she said seriously, lowing her voice so that only Danny and Kay could hear. "Sometimes I wonder whether it's worth all it costs."

"We'll be praying for you," reassured her friends.

"Please do," she replied. Then she smiled quickly and held out her hand to the next in line.

The next day at football practice Danny substituted at the quarter for one series of plays. Then Coach Collins switched him to blocking back.

"You've got the speed to keep out in front of Barton," the coach said. "I believe the two of you will make a good combination.

Tim Barton looked at Danny critically. "You'd better get out in front and move," he said, "or you'll be run over."

"I'll do the best I can."

It was the first time Danny had played blocking back. He found it a little difficult to get used to. On some of the plays he had trouble remembering just where he was supposed to go. Tim kept barking at him about his mistakes until the other half snapped back.

"Lay off him, will you?" Red demanded. "This is the first time Danny's played blocking back. How can you expect him to know what he's supposed to do on all the plays?"

"That's all right, Red," Danny said quickly.

The coach came up just then. "All right, fellows," he said. "Let's get to work. We've got a big game coming up day after tomorrow."

The next play was an end around. Danny was supposed to cut over and lead Tim wide. He started with the snap of the ball, but as he crossed behind tackle he hesitated momentarily. Tim, who had lagged behind purposely, came charging up and hit Danny in the middle of the back, sending him sprawling.

Danny's head whirled. For the moment he couldn't get his breath. The guys crowded about him angrily.

"What was the big idea, Tim?" Red demanded.

"He'll know enough to get out of the way next time!"

Coach Collins went up to the ball carrier. "That was deliberate, Barton! Deliberate and uncalled for."

"I've got to have blockers who can run," Tim answered defensively. "What good are they going to do me if they can't keep up with me?"

"Another deal like that and you won't be needing blockers, Barton. We play together on this team."

Tim started to say something, then stopped, and strode back to his position.

"That will be all for today," the coach said. "There'll be a light drill tomorrow afternoon in sweat clothes. Now I want everybody to go to bed early tonight. And keep those studies up."

When Danny came to school the next morning Coach Collins had one of the guys waiting for him at the front door.

"The coach wants to see you, Danny."

When Danny stepped into the little office, Coach Collins closed the door behind him and went back to his desk.

"I'm glad you held your temper last night, Danny," he said. "I couldn't have blamed you if you hadn't."

"That wouldn't have done any good."

"It could have done a lot of harm," the coach said. He picked up a pencil and fingered it. "I wanted to talk to you about Tim."

Danny sat down.

"I'm afraid that he's going to be a real problem for us. The guys on the team are already choosing sides. He's got his friends who stick up for him and think that everything he does is wonderful. Some of the others are getting so fed up they can't stand him."

"I know," Danny said. "I've heard quite a few of them talking about him."

"We've got a wonderful team. I should say that

we've got the prospects for a wonderful team, providing we all work together. If we let Barton divide us, it can ruin us."

The coach leaned forward. "I'd like to have you and Rick get him into that gang of yours and make him one of you."

"That's a big order."

"It is a big order. A very big order. But the whole future of our season's football team depends on it."

Danny met Rick in the hall at noon and told him what the coach asked them to do. Together they sought out Tim. They found him sitting on the steps in one of the side hallways. Six or eight friends were crowded about him.

"I've got a plaque at home," he was saying, "that shows that I was the best athlete Duluth ever turned out. They offered to pay my tuition and give me spending money and everything if I'd stay there and finish school."

He looked up and saw Danny.

"There's the halfback who can't run. But I'll bet he moves for me from now on! He knows better than to stop and figure out what to do when I'm behind him."

Everyone laughed. Danny felt the color leave his face.

FOUR
The team rebels

"Yes, sir," Tim's voice was loud and arrogant. "I like to have blockers, but they've got to be able to move. When I run, I run. I don't want to be stumbling over somebody."

The guys laughed. In spite of himself Danny's face flushed scarlet. His fists clenched.

"Come on." Rick tugged at his arm. "There's no use trying to make friends with a guy like that."

But Danny Orlis stood there until the laughter died away.

"Are you all set for tomorrow night, Tim?" he asked. "We've got a rough game coming up."

Tim looked at him and honored him with a grin. "Listen," he said, "I've played against Minneapolis South, Milwaukee Teachers, and the Superior Knights. That outfit we're playing tomorrow night seems like a breeze to me."

"They're plenty tough enough for me."

"They won't be so bad this year," the other boy

boasted. "You'll have a real quarterback running things for you."

Rick shook his head as he and Danny walked away.

"Man, oh, man," he said. "Did you ever see anything like that guy? You'd think he invented football!"

"It's going to be awfully hard for us to make friends with him," Danny replied. "We'll have to do an awful lot of praying."

"It sure looks hopeless to me."

They played against Beachwood the following evening. Tim Barton had a field day. Danny blocked him into the open on three successive plays that carried them from their own nine-yard line to the Beachwood twenty-eight. And then, with unerring accuracy he flipped a long pass to Rick who scored standing up.

"Good work," Danny told him as they trotted into position to try for the extra point.

"What did I tell you? These outfits out here are all alike. They're suckers for a good quarterback. We're going to have an undefeated season if I don't get hurt."

That first touchdown gave the guys confidence and they scored again in the first quarter and once more in the second. When the game finally ended after the reserves had played from midway in the third quarter to the final gun, the score stood at a demoralizing 38 to 0. Beachwood had made only two first downs.

"You fellows played a good game," the coach told them in the dressing room. "There's no need to tell you that. But we've got seven more games to play. You've got to dig every minute if we're going to have a good season."

Tim said nothing, but a superior little smile came to the corners of his mouth.

Danny waited until Tim had finished his shower and dressed.

"Well, Tim." Danny walked out into the warm night air with him. "You played a terrific game. And I was able to stay out of your way."

"If you hadn't missed that block in the second quarter I'd have scored another touchdown. What was the matter with you? You had a perfect chance to get him!"

"Maybe you could give me a few pointers," Danny said seriously. "You've played under some topnotch coaches."

"You ask me again sometime. If I'm not busy, I just might do that." Then he walked across the street and left Danny standing there.

The next evening Danny went over to help Kay plan a party for the Young People's Society. When they had selected the games and refreshments and settled on a speaker, Danny talked to her about Tim.

"Isn't he a wonderful football player?" Kay asked.

"He's good, all right. Just about as good as any football player I ever saw, but the trouble is that he knows it."

"That isn't good." Kay pursed her lips thoughtfully.

"It certainly isn't," he answered. "Some of the guys are getting so they can't stand him. If they don't like him they won't block for him like they should, and he'll be tackled before he gets a chance to move."

"What can we do about it?"

"I don't know whether we can do anything," Danny told her. "Our only chance is to get him to Young People's and church and Bible club. He needs the Lord, Kay."

She nodded in agreement. "I don't believe he's very happy. Have you noticed how alone he seems to be, even when there's a gang around him?"

"But why won't he let a guy be friendly with him? Rick and I have tried, but he actually turns and walks away from us."

Kay said nothing. Instead, she took a little notebook out of her purse and scribbled something on it.

"Now what's that for?"

"I was just putting Tim on my prayer list," she said. "We might not know what to do about it, but we don't want to forget that God does."

"That reminds me," Danny said, "what about Marilyn Forester? Did you get a chance to talk to her?"

"She's having an awfully hard time." Kay's voice was sorrowful. "Mrs. Forester isn't going to rest until she has Marilyn dancing and playing cards and running with the country club set."

"No wonder she feels downhearted and discouraged."

"Her mother planned to send her to a private school in the east this fall," Kay went on. "A place where the girls have to dance and do a lot of things that a Christian feels it's better not to do. But Marilyn was able to talk her out of it—for now at least."

"Now that would be something!"

"I'm awfully worried about her." Kay ran her fingers through her soft blond hair. "She told me the other day that she is so tired of fighting, that she's about ready to give in. She said it would be so much easier to do what her mother wanted her to and quit trying to live for Christ."

"We can't let her do that," Danny Orlis said quickly.

"We've got to encourage her to stand up for what she believes. We've got to help her, Kay."

"I know that," she answered. "But how?"

Danny walked home slowly after leaving Kay. Before going to bed, he knelt for a long while praying about Tim and Marilyn. Things were so terribly mixed up for both of them.

"Did you see what the papers had to say about me?" Tim turned to Danny and whispered under his breath, as they were listening to the coach the next day. "Said I was the best quarterback ever to play with Cedarton. And I've only played one game. Just wait until I get the kind of support I ought to have, if I ever do. I'll really show you all some football."

Two or three of the linemen who were sitting close by overheard what he said and glared at him. Why did Tim have to make it so hard for everybody to like him?

Coach Collins finished his lecture presently, and sent them out to scrimmage.

One of the tackles waited for Danny and trotted onto the field with him. "We all got together this noon and decided to give 'loud mouth' a lesson."

Danny looked quizzical.

"What do you mean?"

"Barton's been blowing about doing everything alone. Some of us decided to let him try it that way tonight, and see how he likes it."

"That's no good," Danny countered. "We're a team. We can't pick on one guy like that. The first thing we know we'll be fighting among ourselves. Then we won't be able to beat anyone."

Bill Webster scowled. "If he gets pasted a few times about twenty yards behind the line of scrimmage he'll appreciate it when somebody throws a block to get him in the clear."

"That won't do any good. We don't care what he says. We want to win games."

But Bill Webster was unconvinced. "I want to see him get knocked on his ear a few times. Then he'll find out what it's like to have a good line ahead of him."

Danny wanted to answer him, but there was no opportunity. The coach blew his whistle sharply and sent them into a scrimmage.

As usual, Tim carried the ball on the first play, Bill Webster looked back at Danny from his tackle position and winked significantly. The instant the ball was snapped the B team linemen swarmed through to smack Tim to the ground before he had a chance to move. Coach Collins, who had turned aside to talk to the sports reporter for the local paper, didn't see what had happened.

Tim got to his feet, sputtering. "All right!" he retorted angrily. "Let's try that play again. And you guys in the line! Let's see you play your positions for a change."

The same thing happened a second time, and then a third. The guys in the line crouched and lunged forward as the ball was snapped, but somehow they missed their blocks completely and the whole B team filtered through to pounce on Tim.

"You guys are laying down on the job," Tim stormed. "How do you expect me to get going if you don't take out your men?"

"From the way you talk," Bill said, straight faced, "you don't need anyone to block for you. You can take out the opposition by yourself!"

"With a bunch of lunkheads like you in the line it looks like I'll have to!"

Coach Collins had finished with the reporter by this time and turned his attention back to the scrimmage.

The guys tried to play their positions like they should, but something was missing. The plays came off raggedly. There were several serious fumbles in the backfield, the sort of fumbles that can lose a hard-fought game.

Coach Collins fell in beside Danny as they walked to the dressing room after practice.

"I saw the guys letting Tim get smeared," he said. "And I let it go on for a little while. Figured maybe it would help to take him off his pride a little. But things are getting in bad shape. If things keep on, we won't even have a team."

Danny dressed and started home when he remembered that he had forgotten his history book in the locker. When he went back after it, he was surprised to see someone sitting on one of the benches in the dark. He switched on the light.

Tim jumped to his feet, his eyes blazing. "What are you doing here?" he demanded.

Then Danny saw that his eyes were red and a tear trickled down his cheek.

FIVE
Calling the plays

For an instant Tim glared at Danny. When Tim spoke his voice was harsh and belligerent. "What are you doing here? What's the big idea, anyway?"

"I forgot my history book." Danny acted as though he hadn't seen the tears. "Thought I'd better come back and get it. We're going to have a quiz tomorrow, and I haven't cracked a book for two or three days."

"Well, get it and get out of here!"

"About ready to go? I'll go with you."

"No, I'm not ready to go home," he answered savagely. "And when I do get ready, I'll go alone. I don't need you!" Then he paused, and momentarily, his eyes softened. But when he spoke again, his voice was as harsh as ever. "If you know what's good for you, you'll forget everything you've seen here tonight."

"I don't make a habit of telling what I know." Danny started to leave, but turned back. "Tim," he said gently, "can I help you?"

"When I want your help I'll ask for it!"

The Orlis boy looked into Tim's troubled face.

"There's something bothering you," he said. "Wouldn't you like to tell me about it?"

Tim Barton looked up at him. For an instant the mask slipped away and his lips quivered.

"Wouldn't you like to tell me about it?"

Tim swallowed hard and ran his fingers through his tangled hair. "I can't, Danny!" His voice broke.

They went out of the locker room together and down the wide street. Danny tried to talk to Tim as they walked, but he only grunted an answer.

Danny longed to tell Kay what had happened, to ask her advice. But he had promised Tim not to tell anybody.

"Is there any new development with Tim?" she asked the next evening when they were together.

"I can't really answer that," Danny Orlis told her. "But he's making the guys on the squad so mad at him that things are about to explode. We won't even have a team if something isn't done."

"I've been praying for him and for the rest of the team, too." She was silent while the clock struck nine. "If we could just get them to see that they need a Savior. If we could just get them to confess their sins and give their hearts to Christ, we wouldn't have to worry about problems like this."

"I guess that's right," Danny said. "I don't know whether I'll be able to get Tim to come to Bible club, but I'm going to try."

He had hoped that he would be on friendly terms with the young quarterback after the incident in the locker room, but the next morning he was as arrogant as ever.

"Hi," Danny called out warmly.

Tim swaggered across the street. "Just remember what I told you about keeping your big mouth shut," he muttered.

"Listen, fella," Danny told him. "You can trust me. I'm a Christian. If anybody hears about yesterday afternoon it'll have to come from you."

"That's the way it had better be if you know what's good for you."

The football practice didn't go any better that afternoon than it had the day before. The guys didn't deliberately miss their assignments because the coach crouched over them, watching intently.

"Any man who doesn't give his best here in practice can turn in his suit anytime," he had said at the start of the scrimmage. "We're not going to put up with any foolishness."

In spite of that, the practice went poorly. The timing on the new plays was ragged. Two or three of them didn't come off at all. And the fire and spirit that welded them into a team that first game was lacking. They went through the motions, but for some reason their hearts were not in it. The center made several bad passes that would have been deadly in a regular game. And Tim, who was usually as calm as a professional, got his signals mixed and twice fumbled the ball.

"Come on, now, guys," Danny said, chattering. "We can do better than that. We've got to."

"If our hot-shot quarterback could just remember the signals and hang on to the ball maybe we could do something," the center snapped irritably.

"Look who's talking," Tim retorted. His voice rose hotly. "If you'd get the ball back to me the way you ought to I could hang on to it. Nobody could take the passes like you're firing at me without missing some of them."

The center cocked his fist menacingly. "Another crack like that and you'll pick yourself off the ground. All we've heard out of you has been how good you are. We're getting tired of it."

Tim stepped out to meet him. "I don't take that kind of talk from nobody!"

Coach Collins, who had been talking with one of his assistants, suddenly became aware of what was happening and pushed in between them. "We're not going to have any of this!"

"I'm not going to take anything from him!" Tim's voice cracked with anger.

"And I'm not taking anything from him," the center countered.

The coach separated them firmly. "Forget this foolishness and play ball or you can both turn in your suits. Now get with it!"

They glared at one another but went back to their positions.

"All right, Orlis," Tim barked, "we'll try number 21, only you take the ball. We'll see how well you can take a pass from this lousy center."

Number 21 was a fake reverse. The quarterback was to take the ball from the center, fake it to the fullback who came around fast, and dive over tackle. Tim had tried it three times that afternoon and backfired every time.

Now he called signals from Danny's position at halfback. Danny crouched behind the center in T formation. He took the ball, whirled and acted as though he had handed it to the fullback, and dove through the hole at right tackle. It was only open for a second, but that was enough. Danny slipped through the line, eluded one tackler who came charging in, and blasted out into the open. Two or three blockers came out of nowhere to clear the path and Danny was across the goal line for the touchdown.

The guys looked at Danny and grinned.

"That was a good run, Orlis," Coach Collins said, coming up to them. "And a smart play on your part, Barton. You really crossed the B team up with that one. That's quarterbacking."

The practice seemed to go better after that. Tim called Danny Orlis on two more plays and he made one twenty-eight-yard run, and might have been away for a touchdown had one of the blockers blocked out his man.

"I'm going to do something we've never done before," the coach began when they had dressed and were ready to go home that evening. "We've always appointed a captain for every game, but I think we're going to change that this year. We're going to elect one captain to be in charge all season."

As soon as he called for nominations Tim Barton got to his feet. "I nominate Danny Orlis."

Danny looked at him in amazement.

There was a quick second and then silence. Finally, Rick Haines spoke. "I move that the nominations cease and Danny be declared elected."

Coach Collins called Danny to the front and put his arm about his shoulder. "You fellows made a wise choice. In the last two days, I've seen Danny demonstrate outstanding leadership ability. We've got to get to playing together as a team again. And I am convinced that Danny is the fellow to do it."

Danny smiled happily, but without pride. He looked over at Tim who scowled at him.

When he got home that evening, it was almost seven o'clock. He found that Mr. and Mrs. Meyer had gone out to dinner, leaving a lunch for him in the refrigerator. Karen was upstairs in her room, and Kirk and Don Haines, Rick's younger brother, were lying on their stomachs in the front room. Danny ate slowly and started up to his room to study.

"Hi, guys. What are you doing?"

"Reading comics," Kirk replied, without looking up.

"Comics?" Danny echoed. "Where did you get them?"

"They're some old ones that belonged to Ken Meyer," the younger boy said. "We found them up in the attic last night."

"And boy, are they keen!" Don exclaimed. "Look at this one! Man, it's got murder in it and everything!"

Danny sat down and picked up one of the comics from the pile on the floor between the two younger boys. As Don had said, the comic had everything in it.

It was the story of a guy robbing a bank. It told how he did it, how much money he got, and how he shot and killed the police officer who came to arrest him. The next one showed a picture of a girl being dragged by the hair by some hideous green monster with a head like a skull and long bony fingers. Danny shuddered to look at it.

"Do you guys think you ought to be reading these?"

"Sure, they're good."

"You both profess Christ," Danny went on. "There isn't anything very Christian in books like these.

They show plenty of wickedness, but that's about all."

"But Danny," Kirk protested. "All the kids in school have them. The Christian kids too. They won't hurt us. I just like to read these scary ones for fun."

"How many comics have you read today?" Danny asked him.

"About a dozen, maybe."

"How many chapters have you read from the Bible today?"

A queer look came over Kirk's face. "I've been kind of forgetting my Bible reading lately," he said lamely.

Danny intended to say more, but the doorbell rang and Kirk went to answer it.

"It's for you, Danny."

When the the young Orlis boy went to the door, he saw Tim Barton standing there, his face pale and drawn. "I've got to talk to you, Danny!" he said, his voice hoarse. "I've got to talk to you alone."

SIX
A decision in the night

"Why sure," Danny said, smiling. "Come on in."

Tim's lower lip was trembling. He took a step toward the door, and paused. "Let's go for a walk."

Danny slipped into a light jacket, told Kirk that he would be back in a little while, and stepped outside. The two boys went out to the sidewalk together, and walked half a block up the dark street before either of them said a word.

"I suppose you think I'm silly," Tim said suddenly. A little of the old harshness came back into his voice. "But I—I've just got to talk to somebody. And I found out the other day that you can keep your mouth shut."

Danny said nothing.

They crossed the street and turned toward the business district. "It's about my folks," Tim blurted. "They're getting a divorce!"

"That's too bad!"

"When I got home after practice tonight, Dad was gone," Tim went on, dully. "He'd packed up all his stuff and pulled out."

Danny looked at him rather helplessly.

The star quarterback swallowed hard. For an instant he could not go on.

"They haven't been getting along for a couple of years," he said at last. "All they think about is card playing and dancing and drinking. They don't care what happens to me or to themselves either."

"I'm sure they do care about you, Tim," Danny protested. "They might not show it because these other things—these sins—are in the way. But I'm sure that they think an awful lot of you."

There was a long silence.

"Do you know something?" Tim said in a choked voice. "During all the years I've been playing football, do you know how many times my dad has come to see me play? Once. And that was last year when I got that little chunk of metal that said that I was the best football player that Duluth ever had."

Danny was beginning to understand many things about Tim, things that made him desperately sorry for his teammate. All that "blowing" about how good a football player he was, all the arrogance and conceit he kept showing was just a shell to hide the fact that Tim was actually miserably unhappy and alone.

"What can I do, Danny?" he asked.

"I just don't know," Danny told him. "I wouldn't know whether there would be any possible way for you to get your folks together again. But I can tell you how to get strength and courage to face whatever comes."

A hard glint came into Tim's eyes. "I can get along all right. I've gotten used to taking care of myself."

"You can get along," Danny agreed. "But you aren't"

happy. God has a remedy for that. He can give you strength and courage and happiness, even though everything doesn't go to suit you."

"What do you mean?"

By this time they had reached the park in the courthouse square. Danny sat down on one of the benches and Tim sat down beside him.

"The Bible tells us that if we confess our sins and put our trust in Christ, he will give us eternal life and watch over us and help us from day to day.

"I don't get you," Tim said. "What's that got to do with happiness and all those other things?"

"It's sort of hard for me to explain," Danny told him. "I don't know my Bible well enough to tell you the exact verses, but I know from experience that it's true. I've had things happen to me that would have been hard to take if I hadn't had the Lord to trust. And I know a lot of other Christians who have found the same thing to be true."

Tim took a deep breath. "I don't know what you're driving at. I never did go to Sunday school and church. The folks were always too tired after Saturday night to get up before noon."

Danny got out his Testament and began to read to Tim in the dim light of the street lamp above them. He read the story of Nicodemus, how a person had to be born again before he could go to heaven, and explained how he had to put his trust in Christ.

"But why does everyone have to have a Savior?" Tim broke in. "Why couldn't a guy just live good enough so that he could go to heaven?"

"The Bible tells us that we've all sinned and come short of the glory of God. Nobody can live good enough to be saved, that's why we have to have a Savior."

Tim stared blankly.

"Think just a minute," Danny said. "Do you honestly believe that you could go for just one day and do everything perfectly? You wouldn't say anything to hurt anyone. You wouldn't think anything wrong. You wouldn't do a single thing that you wouldn't want God to know about. Do you think you could do it?"

There was a short silence.

"Not me," Tim said truthfully.

As they talked he asked a hundred questions. Danny tried to answer them, but somehow his answers weren't enough.

"I'll tell you this much," Tim said, getting to his feet, "someday I'm going to. But I want to think about it for a while, first."

That was all Danny could do for him. Tim held out his hand, "Thanks, Danny." His voice choked. "You're the first real friend I've ever had."

"Put this Testament of mine in your pocket. I've marked some verses that might help you."

When Danny reached home he went to the phone and called Kay. "I can't tell you much about it over the phone," he said, "but I've just spent the evening talking with Tim, talking to him about the Lord."

"That's wonderful," Kay exclaimed. "Is he saved?"

"Not yet," he told her. "But he did listen. He needs our prayers, Kay."

Danny found himself waking two or three times during the night, he was so disturbed about Tim. Each time he prayed for his unhappy teammate, but there seemed to be no answer.

The next morning when Danny finished breakfast and started to school, he was surprised to see Tim waiting for him in the front yard.

"Hi. Remember me?"

"Hi, Tim," Danny fell in beside him and they started toward the school together.

"Well," Tim said, smiling, "it happened."

"What do you mean?"

"After I got home last night I took that Bible you gave me," he explained. "I read about half of the night. When I awoke early this morning I read some of those verses you had marked. I finally understood what you were trying to tell me. So I knelt beside the bed and confessed that I was a sinner and prayed that I'd put my trust in Jesus." He paused a moment. "A guy can do that, can't he?"

"Sure you can," Danny assured him. "The Lord will hear you anywhere."

"I don't feel so much different. Should I?"

"It's a matter of trusting," Danny replied. "It isn't a matter of feeling."

Danny and Tim didn't have any classes together and Danny didn't see his new Christian friend until they went out onto the football field that afternoon for practice.

"We're going to have a short scrimmage tonight," Coach Collins told them. "We don't want to get anybody hurt. We've got to be at full strength if we want to beat Remington."

The first string took the ball on their own twenty-yard line and Tim barked out the signals. As the ball was passed back to him, Bill Webster let the second team tackle sift through to nail Tim before he could get underway.

The quarterback jumped to his feet, his eyes flashing. "Of all the dumb playing!" he exclaimed angrily. "What's the matter with you, Bill? Are you afraid to block?" He stopped abruptly and a peculiar look came over his face. He stood there momentarily. "I–I'm sorry, fella. Let's try it again."

Bill stared at him in amazement.

The practice went better than it had for days. The line snapped into position like a college outfit. They surged forward as one man the instant the ball was snapped. Plays that had been ragged and bungling the night before were executed sharply. The A team marched from their own twenty across the B squad's line in less than a dozen plays.

"That's it, fellows," Coach Collins called without trying to conceal his satisfaction. "Go to your showers, get in early tonight, and we'll show Remington they've got a game on their hands."

He called Danny over to him. "You've done wonders with those fellows. I don't see how you got them to play so well together. Last night they were at each other's throats."

"It isn't anything that I've done," Danny replied. "It's Tim."

"Tim?" Collins echoed.

"I'd rather he told you, coach," Danny said, respectfully.

The next evening Cedarton played Remington. It was a hard, bruising game against a rugged team that hadn't been defeated for two straight seasons.

Remington rolled up a fast touchdown in the opening minutes of the first quarter and buckled down determinedly to force Cedarton to punt.

On the first two plays the fullback bucked the line for no gain. On the third, Tim faked an end run around. He dropped back rapidly, flipped a long, flat pass to Rick on the far sidelines. He scooped in the ball and scampered across the midfield stripe and down to the Remington eighteen. The crowd went wild.

"All right, guys," Tim said in the huddle. "Let's give them number 21 with Danny carrying the ball."

His teammates looked at him in surprise. Always before, even in practice, when they got down close to the goal line, they could know that Tim would carry the ball himself. Remington must have learned that from their scouting. They swarmed on him, not even noticing Danny until he was away for the touchdown.

After that there was no stopping Cedarton. They scored again in the second and twice in the third period against the stubborn Remington line. And during the same period they held the league champions scoreless. When the game finally ended they had swamped Remington 27 to 6.

Coach Collins was lavish with praise in the locker room after the game. "You met and beat a mighty good team tonight," he said. "You played better football than I ever thought you could." He turned to Tim. "You did all right, Barton," he said. "I liked the way you used the other fellows, as well as yourself to carry the ball."

"Yeah," Bill Webster said loudly. "What came over

you last night and tonight, Tim? You played like you were one of us. What happened to 'our' hero?"

The guys all looked toward the star quarterback. His face paled and Danny saw that his lower lip trembled nervously.

SEVEN
Difficult assignment

"Listen, guys," Danny spoke quickly. "Lay off Tim. He played a terrific game."

"You'd better take your showers and head for home," Coach Collins broke in. "We've got a tough game coming up next week, and we've got to stay in shape."

"I was just kidding," Bill said. "I didn't mean anything by it."

Some of the guys had started to peel out of their football togs when Tim spoke. "I don't mind telling you guys what happened," he said, slowly. "It'll probably sound crazy to you, but I–I've accepted Christ as my Savior. That's why I've been different the past two or three days."

A hush settled over the locker room.

"For the first time in my life, I got wise to myself. I saw what a dope I was to live the way I have been. I read in the Bible that I needed to be saved." He took a deep breath. "I want to apologize to you for the way I treated you. I felt terrible, even when I was doing it.

But I guess I was so proud and wanted to be so important that I had to keep boasting."

There was a strained, embarrassed silence. Coach Collins tugged at the lobe of his ear and a strange, quizzical look came into his eyes.

"I wish I could tell you guys how different everything is." Tim grew bolder as he spoke. "I wish I could tell you how wonderful it is to know that you've met Christ's conditions and have been—have been saved."

With that he stopped, embarrassed suddenly by what he had done.

Coach Collins walked over and put his arm on the young quarterback's shoulder. "I just want you to know that I'm for you, Tim. What you've done just now takes a lot of nerve." He turned back to the squad. "If I hear one of you make a crack about this, if I hear one of you razz him, you're through; you can turn in your suit."

And then the guys began to drift to the showers. Rick and Danny came over and thanked Tim for giving his testimony.

"I tried to keep still," he told them. "I was afraid the guys'd laugh at me. But I couldn't. Christ died on the cross for me. The least I can do for him is to tell people about it and let them know that he saved me."

After they had their showers and got dressed, Danny and Tim walked home together.

"It was wonderful the way you testified tonight," Danny said. "A lot of people who've been Christians for years haven't had the courage to speak out for Jesus that way."

"I've told the gang on the squad that I've taken

Christ as my Savior," Tim said at last, "but there's someone else I haven't told yet."

"Who's that?" Danny asked.

"My mother," he answered hesitantly.

"It ought to be easier for you to tell her now," Danny said, "after you've testified to the guys. That's one thing about testifying. It gets easier every time you do it."

"But you don't know Mother."

"It's a job that won't get any easier if you let it go. And you might be able to win her for Christ."

"Do you really think so?"

"We'll pray that she will become a Christian, Tim. The Bible tells us that God hears and answers our prayers."

"I think she's home now," the star quarterback said. "Would you pray for me if I—I mean while I go home and—and talk to her?"

Danny Orlis prayed faithfully as he walked across town to the Meyers' home where he stayed.

"Is that you, Danny?" Kirk called from the kitchen. "Come on out and have a cookie and a glass of milk."

"Sounds good." Danny went into the kitchen.

"Boy, that was some game you guys played tonight. That Tim's a terrific quarterback."

"You can say that again. And the best part of it is he's taken Christ as his Savior. He even gave a testimony to the guys tonight."

A queer look came to Kirk's face.

Danny eyed him closely. "You used to be happy when a friend of yours became a Christian. Is something wrong?"

"Oh, no, no, nothing's wrong," he replied hurriedly.

"It's great that Tim's a Christian. In fact, it's wonderful."

As he spoke, both of them looked across the table at the stack of comic books. Kirk's face colored.

"I was taking them back to the guys I borrowed them from," he ventured lamely.

"I wish you wouldn't read that trash, Kirk," Danny said. "It's so filled with sin and wickedness that it isn't good for anyone, let alone a Christian. It's a hard thing to keep soaking up that stuff and not drift away from the path Christ would have you walk."

Before Kirk could speak, the phone rang and Danny went to answer it. It was Tim.

"Hello, Danny," his voice sounded dull and far away. "I talked to her. I told her how I had put my trust in Jesus and what he meant to me."

There was a long silence. Danny waited for him to go on.

"She didn't say anything," Tim said miserably. "She just laughed."

Danny stood for a time beside the telephone after he and Tim quit talking. It was going to be terribly hard for the new Christian.

The next day was Saturday. Danny had intended to get over to see Tim and ask him to go to Sunday school and church with him Sunday. But Mr. Meyer wanted him to work at the store. Tim wasn't at church, but Danny did get him to go to the Monday night Bible club.

"I can't go to a place like that," Tim protested.

"Why not?"

He spoke reluctantly. "To tell you the truth, I don't

have the clothes to wear. I wanted to go to church yesterday, but you can't go in a pair of faded cords and a sweater." His smile was crooked and without humor. "The liquor store has been getting most of the money around our place for a long time."

"It doesn't make any difference what kind of clothes you wear," Danny told him. "What God cares about is that we meet together to worship him. Your clothes may be faded and old, or not."

"I'll think about it."

"Pray about it, too," Danny Orlis suggested. "That'll do more good."

They had a light drill that afternoon. And that evening Tim went to the Bible club meeting with Danny and Kay. During testimony time he surprised everyone by getting to his feet and giving his testimony.

When the meeting was over the three of them, and Marilyn, stood on the front porch of the house where the meeting had been held.

"Where's Rick?" Kay asked Marilyn.

"Oh, he took Esther Dixon home tonight," she said.

"That's a new development."

"Since last night."

Danny grinned. "What sort of a fight was it?"

"No fight at all," Marilyn answered. "It was nice and peaceable. As a matter of fact, we decided that maybe we've been missing something by going steady."

"Well, in that case," Tim told her, "let's go down and have a dish of ice cream." He took a few cents change out of his pocket. "A small dish, that is."

The four of them went down to the ice cream shop

and found a booth toward the back. "You know," Marilyn said, "I've been having a terrible time with Mother since we had Bible club at our home. She was going to forbid me to run around with any of you kids, or go to Bible club, or your church, or anything. But Dad wouldn't let her."

Tim was concerned immediately. "You and I have the same kind of trouble," he said. He told her then how he talked with his mother about the Lord. "And she just sat there and laughed at me!"

"You'd think our mothers would be happy about it," Marilyn said. "But instead, they act as though we've committed some terrible sin."

"They can't be happy because you've accepted the Lord," Kay put in, "because they aren't believers themselves. They don't know what it is. They're afraid of it."

For a long minute they were silent.

"I'd give anything if I could just lead my folks to Christ," Tim said, more to himself than to the others. "They wouldn't be getting a divorce."

Later, as Danny told Kay good night, he said, "We've got to remember to pray for those kids. They are really going to need it."

Kay bit her lower lip thoughtfully. "If only there was something we could do to help them. Do you suppose it would help if Mrs. Meyer talked to Tim's mother?"

"That's an excellent idea."

Mrs. Meyer agreed to go with Danny to talk to Tim's mother, but with his football practice, and her work at church, they couldn't find time until Saturday afternoon.

60

On Friday night Cedarton walloped Cheston decisively. Coach Collins pulled the regulars midway in the third quarter and left them on the bench for the rest of the game. Already the exploits of the team were being heard as far away as the Twin Cities. The Minneapolis paper had a sports writer at the Cheston game who interviewed both Tim and Danny when it was over.

The next afternoon the Orlis boy and Mrs. Meyer walked out to the edge of town where Tim and his mother lived. The house was small and the paint was cracked and peeling. The screen was half torn from the screen door and the lower step was broken.

Mrs. Barton opened the door suspiciously.

"Who are you?"

"I'm Mrs. Meyer," she said, smiling. "May we come in?"

Tim's mother still blocked the door. "You aren't from the welfare office, are you?"

"No, nothing like that. Danny, here, is a friend of Tim."

She stepped aside reluctantly and held open the door.

She was a thin woman and prematurely gray. It was easy to see that she had once been very pretty. But now there were deep circles under her eyes, and the corners of her mouth sagged with deep weariness.

Danny and Mrs. Meyer sat on the threadbare sofa.

"What do you want to talk to me about?" Mrs. Barton still stood.

"You knew Tim had become a Christian, didn't you?" Mrs. Meyer began.

"He came home telling me a crazy story. That's

what he said he'd done, but I didn't know what he was talking about," she replied, a grim, sardonic smile playing on her face. Then her voice grew cold and bitter. "I can tell you this much. I don't put any stock in it. God never did anything for me except give me a drunken, no good husband who spends his money on booze and gambling. I've got a lot to thank God for, I have."

"I used to feel that way too, Mrs. Barton." Mrs. Meyer spoke gently. "My husband died, leaving me with very little money and two small children to rear. I was so bitter that I didn't want to have anything to do with God. Then Danny talked to me and before long I began to see that I needed a Savior. You'll never know how happy and wonderful it has been for me just to put my trust in him."

Mrs. Barton's face was forbidding. "I'm not going to have you here, preaching to me," she snapped. She strode to the door and opened it. "Get out! And you leave Tim alone, too!"

EIGHT
Trouble ahead

Danny and Mrs. Meyer sat there for a minute or two, stunned by the sudden burst of anger.

"You'd better go now," Mrs. Barton's face was white.

"But we'd like to help you," the boy broke in. "We'd like to have you come to our Sunday school and church with Tim."

"When I want your help, I'll ask for it."

Mrs. Meyer got to her feet. "I know how you feel, Mrs. Barton." Her voice was gentle and understanding. "And I am terribly sorry. I want you to know that we'll be praying for you."

Mrs. Barton's lips began to tremble. "I don't need your prayers. I don't need anything."

When they were outside, Danny turned to Mrs. Meyer. "I'm sorry it happened like this," he said. "I thought maybe we could do something for her and Tim."

But Mrs. Meyer scarcely heard him.

"The poor woman. The poor, bewildered, frightened woman. I'm so glad you took me to see her, Danny. She needs help, desperately."

"We can't help her. She won't let us."

"God can prepare her heart, Danny, the same way he prepared mine."

Back home, Danny tried to study. Still he could not get his mind off his friend Tim. He needed help too. A new Christian, he did not have solid grounding in what he believed. He did not know anything about the Bible. He had not even been going to Sunday school and church. How could he stand firm for Christ? Danny bowed his head at his desk and prayed for Tim, for his mother and his dad.

In spite of the opposition at home, Tim was at Sunday school and church the next morning, wearing a pair of cords Danny had given him.

"Mother told me about your visit yesterday," he said as soon as services were over and they were outside. "I'm sorry for the way she treated you. She's so upset she hardly knows what she's doing."

"I know. But you're the one I've been concerned about. Opposition like you've got at home is going to make things hard."

Tim nodded. Tears came to his eyes momentarily.

They crossed the street. "Don't say anything about it to the other kids, Danny, please. But I've got to talk to someone. Mother talks about Dad gambling and drinking and all. But the truth of the matter is that she—" He stopped and gulped hard. "She drinks and smokes and gambles right along." He bit his lower lip and rubbed another tear from his eye with his fist. "Sometimes I get to the place where I want to leave home and never return. Mother and Dad don't care anything about me. They never did!"

"I know how you feel. But it isn't that your folks don't love you. They're blinded by sin, that's all. You know, Tim, the wonderful thing about salvation is that it doesn't make any difference how much we've sinned, or what our sin has been. If we recognize that we've done wrong and pray for forgiveness and put our trust in the Lord Jesus, it's all wiped out, as though it had never happened."

Tim smiled hopefully.

"Keep on praying, with faith, believing that God will save them. Then don't try to force your faith on them. But every time you get an opportunity, talk to them about the Lord."

The following Friday evening, the football team squeaked past nearby Clarinda, Minnesota, in a game that looked, for the first three quarters, as though Cedarton was going down to defeat. The Clarinda line was powerful and big, and Cedarton was hobbled by injuries. Bill Webster was nursing a sprained ankle and Rick, who played next to him at end, had a broken finger.

Their substitutes did the best they could, but they could not keep the charging Clarinda forward wall from sifting through to nail the ball carriers before they could get underway. Clarinda scored in the second quarter, made their kick for the extra point, and settled down to hang on to their narrow lead.

All through the third quarter it looked as though seven points were enough to win for them. But in the opening moments of the fourth quarter, Danny faded back on one of Tim's plays and rifled a short, bullet-fast pass to the quarterback out in the flat. Tim snuggled it in his arm, ducked the outstretched fingers of the nearest tackler, and scampered across the mid-field stripe and the goal line.

That fired the team. They smashed through the surprised Clarinda line with such force on the third play after the kickoff return that the punter kicked the ball almost sideways out of bounds. Cedarton got the ball on the Clarinda twenty-eight-yard line.

"All right, gang!" Tim chanted. "Let's go now!"

He took the ball, faked to the halfback and smashed into the center of the line for nine yards. On the next play he threw a short pass that was complete to the seven-yard line. And on three successive line bucks they drove across the goal line to go out in front. The rest of the game was a bitter, grueling battle between two powerful, dog-tired teams.

"That was great," Coach Collins told them in the locker room when the last gun had sounded. "I'm proud of every one of you."

When Danny and Tim and two or three of the others came out of the locker room a stranger approached them and called to Danny. "Danny!" Danny turned to see Mr. Moore, the athletic director of West Farmington University who had been fishing up at the Angle.

"Hi, I didn't recognize you at first."

"I just wanted to tell you," the athletic director said, "that you played a terrific game tonight."

"Thank you."

"You're everything I thought you'd be and more. I don't want to say anything to you now, but give us a chance to talk to you before you come to a definite decision about a school."

"I'll certainly do that."

"Fine," the man replied. "And Danny, don't mention to anyone that I talked with you tonight, please."

"I won't say anything," he agreed.

His heart was hammering in his throat as he joined the others. To think that he was going to have a chance to play football with a big-name school, with one of the teams they always considered when selecting players for the All-American lists.

Tim had asked Marilyn to go with him, Danny, and Kay for a sandwich and ice cream after the game. They went down to the ice cream shop where the gang usually congregated and sat in a booth eating and reliving every moment of the hard-fought game.

"If we can just get Rick and Bill back in there before we have to play Fairview, we'll be all right," Danny said. "I'll tell you, that's going to be the tough game, and it's the very last one of the season."

"If the guys all play together," Tim put in confidently, "we'll put Fairview away. They aren't so bad."

It was quite late when they left the ice cream shop and Tim walked home with Marilyn. When she went into the house she was surprised to see her mother sitting in the living room, busy with one of her endless party lists.

"Hello, Marilyn," she said, looking up. "Did you go to the mixer tonight after the game?"

"No, I didn't, Mother," she replied. The reason had been that the kids always danced there, but she didn't explain that to her mother. It would only cause trouble.

"Where's Daddy?" Marilyn asked.

"Oh, he's working at the office again tonight," her mother said carelessly. "Sit down a minute, dear.

There's something I want to talk to you about."

She sat down dutifully in a chair on the other side of the handsomely furnished room.

"It's been such a long time since you've had a party, Marilyn," she began, checking a name off her list. "Wouldn't you like to entertain some of your friends?"

"But, Mother," Marilyn protested, "there are so many parties at school and church and Young People's that I don't know how we'd have time for any more."

"I know," Mrs. Forester replied curtly. "But you aren't associating with the proper young people. I want you to get in with the right group, darling, and have good times with them. You're missing out on so much this year. Your father and I have had such big plans for you."

"But I'm happy, Mother," she said. "Happier than I've ever been."

"I've decided on a party," Mrs. Forester snapped. "It's going to be a big party out at the club, the sort of a party I'd have given anything to have had when I was a girl."

"But I don't want a party."

"We're going to have a party, my dear. And you are going to be there and take part. I simply won't have this fanatic religion you've gotten mixed up in ruining the happiest days of your life. One of these times you'll come to your senses and be heartbroken over what you've missed."

Tears came to Marilyn's eyes, but she said nothing.

The game with Clarinda set the Cedarton team on fire. Although they were still without the services of the injured end and tackle, they rolled over their next two opponents without difficulty. Championship talk was in the air and sports writers freely predicted that the Cedarton eleven could out-point any squad in the state.

"I don't want you fellows to get conceited," the coach cautioned. "We know that only two of the teams we've met so far have really been up to their average strength. I just talked with the doctor and he said that we will have Bill and Rick back with us for our next game. If we don't have any more injuries, and if we don't have any of you fall by the wayside because of poor grades, we've got a good chance of winning our two remaining games."

He looked over the squad slowly and Tim winced.

Later, when they were outside, Danny said, "I wonder who he was talking about being down in his grades? Boy, that could ruin us."

"I guess I'd just as well tell you," Tim said. "It's me."

"You?" Danny echoed. "But I thought you got good grades all the time. What happened?"

"I did get good grades," Tim countered, "but the truth of the matter is that I didn't earn them. There were always kids who would work my lessons for me, or let me copy, especially in math." He stopped a moment. "I hate to tell you this, Danny, but I never did learn the fundamentals of algebra. After I became a Christian, I knew I couldn't keep on cheating the way I'd been doing. And to tell you the truth, I've been having an awful time."

Danny pursed his lips thoughtfully. "Boy," he exclaimed, "we've got to do something! If you don't play, we're sunk!"

NINE
The keys to victory

That evening was Bible club meeting night. Even
though Tim had been having a great deal of trouble
with his algebra, he took time from his studying to go
to the meeting. Danny called him after dinner, but
the star quarterback had already gone.

"I don't know where he went," Mrs. Barton said. "He
spent an hour or so talking on the phone to some of
his friends. I don't know where he was going, and I
didn't ask him what time he'd be back."

When Danny got to Bible club, Tim was already
there. And with him were six classmates who had
never attended before.

"Hi, Danny," he sang out. "I called some more of the
guys, but they had something planned. Got a couple
or three more who promised to come next time,
though."

"That's great!"

There was a large number of new kids that night.
The lesson seemed to go better than it had since the
beginning of the school year. Some of Tim's enthusi-

asm seemed to rub off on the rest of the members.

"We've got to get out and bring in new kids," Tim said as the meeting drew to a close. "I got to thinking about it in school today. Jesus did so much for me, I've got to do something for him. One thing I can do is to invite my friends to these meetings."

"You know," Danny said as he and Kay and Marilyn and Tim sat and talked after the Bible club meeting, "you made me ashamed of myself tonight, Tim. I've hardly asked anyone to come to Bible club this year."

"I've been the same way," Kay confessed. "And I didn't think much about it before tonight when I saw that gang of guys you rounded up."

"The trouble is," Danny said, "we get into our own tight little groups and stay there. We almost act like we don't care about anyone else. We've got to talk to the kids about Christ. We've got to get them out to Bible club and Young People's and to church."

"We ought to let this be a lesson to us," Marilyn put in. "If each of us had brought as many kids as Tim did, just think of the crowd we would have had."

"Believe me," Danny said fervently, "I'm going to have at least one guest at the next meeting."

"After the football season is over you might have a little more time to do some inviting," Kay said.

"As far as I'm concerned," Tim put in seriously, "the football season may already be over."

"What do you mean?" The girls spoke as one.

Sorrowfully he told them how much trouble he was having with his algebra. "I've got a bunch of back assignments," he concluded, "and two tests to make up if I'm going to play either this week or next. I tell you I'm in a jam."

"We'll all make it a real matter of prayer," Kay told him.

"I'm certainly going to need it. My trouble is I haven't mastered the fundamentals of algebra the way I should have. And when I take a test and don't copy from the guy sitting next to me, I'm just lost."

"Would you like to have me help you a little with it, Tim?" Marilyn asked. "Math is my major."

"Would I!" he exclaimed. "When do we start?"

"You come over to the house tomorrow evening, and bring your algebra along."

Tim grinned happily. "I knew I needed help," he said, "but I certainly didn't know where I was going to get it."

Tim's mother was asleep when he got home that evening, but the next morning when he was eating breakfast she asked where he had been.

"A couple of mothers called," she said, "and wanted to know what kind of a club you had invited their sons to attend."

"I asked them to go to Bible club with me. We get together once a week to sing choruses and hymns and study the Bible."

Mrs. Barton poured a cup of coffee for herself and sat down. "I suppose Mrs. Meyer and that Danny whatever-his-name-is got you into it."

"Mrs. Meyer didn't have anything to do with it," Tim replied. "But Danny did get me to go. He's been talking to me about living a good Christian life and things like that."

"Well, he'd better leave you alone," she retorted angrily. "Coming over here like he was so high and mighty—so much better than we are. I'm not going to have it."

"But Mother," Tim protested. "Danny and Mrs. Meyer didn't mean any harm. They just came to talk to you about the Lord Jesus Christ. They wanted to help us."

"We don't need any help from the likes of them!" She got to her feet and paced across the room. "I don't want you to have anything to do with people like that, Tim. Stay away from them!"

He looked at her. "If you forbid me to have anything to do with Danny," he said gently, "I'll stay away from him. But I've got the Lord Jesus in my heart. I couldn't forsake him."

Her hands were trembling as she went back and sat down. "Well," she said at last, "you can run with this Danny character if you want to, but he'd better not come around here preaching to me! That's all I can say!"

Tim's heart was aching as he got his jacket on and went to school.

When he went out for football that night the coach came over to talk to him about algebra.

"I'm really going to work on it," he answered him. "I've got someone to help me, and I'm going to get it made up in the next few days."

"That's fine, Tim. I'm not too concerned about this game Friday, but the game with Benson Lake has me worried. They've scouted us for the last three games. They ought to know our plays as well as we do. I'm working on some new ones that center around you, Tim. We're going to use the T formation."

"We used the T at Duluth," he said.

"I know that. I talked with your former coach by phone last night. But this algebra thing can cause us real trouble. We don't have another man on the squad who's had any experience with the T. If we work up those plays, we're going to have to count on you."

"You get the plays," Tim said with determination. "I'll take care of my algebra."

That evening, as soon as the star quarterback had finished supper, he gathered his books and hurried over to Marilyn's. They went out into the kitchen and went to work. It helped a great deal for Tim to have someone to explain the fundamentals he should have gotten the year before.

"I'm beginning to see a little light on some of this stuff," he said when they quit studying about nine-thirty. "Two or three more nights, and I believe that I'll be able to take those tests."

When he had gone, Mrs. Forester came into the kitchen.

"Who was that young man?"

"He's Tim Barton, a new boy in school. He's our star quarterback and he's having a little trouble with his algebra. So I'm coaching him."

"I see." Mrs. Forester wrinkled her nose. "He wasn't dressed very well."

"I'm afraid they don't have much money. He's living with his mother and they have a hard time getting along."

"Is his father dead?" she probed.

"They're divorced," Marilyn told her, "or they are going to be. Anyway, his dad left."

"Well, I guess that isn't anything out of the ordinary," she said. "Divorces don't mean what they used to." She paused a moment. "But of course you wouldn't expect to invite him to your party. After all, with his background and everything I'm just afraid that he wouldn't fit in with the other young folks."

"But Mother," Marilyn protested. "I don't want to have a party without my friends. And Tim is a friend of mine."

"It is time," Mrs. Forester said icily, "that you start to do something about those so-called friends of yours."

Marilyn looked at her a moment, as though she wanted to speak, then turned back to her studies.

"I have all the plans completed for your party," her mother said. "We'll all go out to the country club the night after the last football game."

Tim Barton worked hard on his algebra the next few days. He made up most of his back work and one test, but he still had more to do before he could get his grade up enough to play football. He missed the first game, but the algebra teacher assured him that if he did as well on the balance of his work he would be eligible to play in the all-important contest with Benson Lake.

The new plays were ideal for Cedarton's hard charging line and nimble-footed Tim Barton.

Fever for the game with Benson Lake was running high. The town had been excited about it for the past week. At school they dismissed classes at ten o'clock in the morning and held a big, impromptu rally. Two or three businessmen spoke and the student body got so excited that they finally dismissed classes for the balance of the day.

The day of the game had awakened dark and gray, with low, overhanging clouds and a chill north wind.

By noon it started to rain a little, an unseasonable rain that hinted of worse weather to come. In the afternoon the rain turned to snow.

"Boy," Tim said to Danny as they stood in the doorway at school and watched the snow sift down, "I hate to see this change in the weather. It's going to make it rough on us out there tonight."

"I do too," Danny answered. "I hate to play in the rain or snow. A guy can't get good enough footing to get any plays underway. But it'll be just as wet and disagreeable for Benson Lake as it will for us. That's one good thing."

"I'm not so sure. With the T formation we'll really be handicapped on a wet field. To tell you the truth, I have all kinds of trouble in the mud."

TEN
Showdown

Snow continued to fall all afternoon, a soft, slushy snow that soaked up the ground and churned into a dirty gray on the streets of Cedarton. It came down like a curtain of white until it hid the trees and blotted out the sharp outlines of the houses that lined the streets.

Since classes had been dismissed for the day, most of the students stood silently at the school windows and watched the snow.

"We can never play football in this stuff," Tim said when it was still snowing at four o'clock.

"Maybe they'll postpone it," someone said.

"That's a hard thing to do," Danny answered. "We could have snow on the ground all winter long. We might not get to play Benson Lake unless we play them tonight."

The school authorities felt that way too. They had several consultations during the day. And when it finally quit snowing about five-thirty, they decided to go ahead.

The stands at the football field began to fill at seven o'clock. By the time the crew had the muddy field cleared of snow, the fans had crowded the bleachers and spilled over onto the oval track that circled the football field.

It was a grueling, bitterly fought game from the very beginning. The two elevens battled back and forth across the center of the field for two full quarters, churning it to a quagmire.

Neither team could execute any of their fast, dazzling plays. Linemen slipped and fell flat as they charged forward. Backfield men stumbled and dropped the ball as they spun on reverses or tried to drive around end. The game was hard fought and without score until the dying moments of the second quarter. Then Tim attempted a punt on his own twelve-yard line. The wet, slippery ball skidded off his foot and went dribbling to the fourteen-yard line where a Benson Lake tackle pounced on it. The Benson Lake coach sent in the regular quarterback who had been resting on the sidelines and the team surged to life.

In three running plays they slipped and skidded down to the two-yard line for a first down. And in two more grimly determined line bucks, they punched across for the touchdown. They missed the try for the point, but that was small consolation to the weary, mud-splattered Cedarton eleven as they left the field at the half.

"We're behind six points," Coach Collins told them in the locker room, "but we aren't any worse off than we were before. It still takes only one touchdown to win and we're going to do that. You've got to forget about the mud and start playing football."

Out on the field a few minutes later, Danny said, "Tim, when we get the ball, why don't we try a few passes."

"You mean pass in this goo?" the star quarterback demanded. "That would be suicide, wouldn't it?"

"That's just what Benson will be thinking," Danny went on. "And they won't be expecting us to pass." He took hold of Tim's arm and pointed to the grassy strip along the west sidelines. "Now we haven't played over in there very much and the footing is pretty good. Let's try to work the ball over that way and try a couple of passes as soon as we can."

Cedarton received the kickoff at the beginning of the third quarter and ran the ball back to their thirty-five-yard line. On the next play, Tim had Danny carry the ball around the end on a play that made little yardage, but set them up near the grass.

"OK, Danny," Tim whispered. "We'll try number 13 with you receiving."

"You're going to pass?" a couple of the guys said in dismay.

But Danny had already broken up the huddle and Tim began to bark out signals. The crowd moaned as Tim dropped back rapidly and shot a flat, soft pass out behind the Benson end. Danny gathered it in, his legs driving like pistons. He scooted past the surprised Benson Lake secondary and would have scored had he not slipped and fallen on the Benson Lake eighteen-yard line.

"All right," Tim snapped in the huddle. "Number 13 again."

It worked a second time as well as it had the first.

Danny drove to the four-yard line. This time there was no stopping them. On the next play the fullback crashed over the center for a touchdown. They missed the point, but it did not matter. They scored another touchdown in the third quarter and a third in the dying moments of the game to win 20 to 6.

When the guys finally made their way through the crowd of well wishers after the game and got dressed, Danny and Tim ducked out of the locker room and down the corridor to the outer door.

"Everything worked out OK," Tim said happily. "Even if I did just about give it away with that bum kick."

At the ice cream shop everyone was talking about the game and the league championship.

Tim and Danny walked over to the booth where Marilyn and Kay were sitting.

"You two fellows looked more like college players out there tonight than you did high school boys," a tall man interrupted, stepping up to the booth.

Danny looked up to see Glen Moore, athletic director of West Farmington U, standing at their table. He was with the Cedarton man who had just spoken to them.

"And I'd like to tell you again, Danny," Mr. Moore said, smiling, "that I want very much to talk to you and your friend here before you make up your mind where you are going to school next year. I know we can make a place for both of you."

"Who was that guy?" Tim asked when Mr. Moore left.

His eyes opened wide when Danny told him. "You mean he wants us to go to West Farmington U and play football with them?" he asked excitedly. "Boy, wouldn't that be something!"

"I could hardly believe it when he first talked to me." Danny then told them how Mr. Moore had approached him at Angle Inlet. "It would give us a real chance to go to college cheap. And we could be a testimony, too."

"Of course," Kay put in softly, "the important thing for all of us in choosing a school is to go where the Lord wishes us. The Bible says, 'Seek ye first the kingdom of God.'"

Danny was silent for a moment. "I guess you're right at that."

Somebody else came up to talk to them. When he had gone, Tim said, "I was just wondering why we don't get together tomorrow night and sort of celebrate our victory? I haven't been to a good party for ages."

"Sounds like fun," Danny and Kay said.

Marilyn's face clouded. "I–I'm sorry," she said hesitantly, "but I can't. I'm having a party tomorrow night."

The others looked at her queerly. "That's all right," Tim said, laughing. "We'll all come to your party."

Her face flushed scarlet. "What I meant," she said at last, "was that my mother's having the party for me out at the country club. She's invited the guests and planned everything."

Concern was quick to show on Kay's face. "Oh, I'm sorry," she said.

Marilyn shook her head. "Mother's determined that I'm going to run with the kids she wants me to run with," she said, "and do the things she wants me to do."

"We'll be praying for you, Marilyn," Kay said simply.

The following day Mrs. Forester began buzzing from the country club to the caterer's to the florist's and back again.

"I'm so excited, my dear," she bubbled to Marilyn as she came to a stop long enough to nibble a few bites of lunch at noon. "This is going to be the most glorious party you've ever had. I know that when it's over you're going to say you've never had so much fun in all your life. You'll forget silly notions about not dancing and having a good time. You'll see that there isn't a thing wrong in having fun."

"I'll go to the party, Mother," Marilyn agreed. "And I'll try to be friendly and have a good time, but I—I just can't dance!"

Her mother bristled. "Can't dance?" she echoed. "Don't be absurd! You have guests coming. You have to dance with them. I insist!"

"But Mother!" she protested.

"I'll hear no more about it! I've been working for two solid weeks on this party. I've been saving it as a surprise for you, but I've engaged a splendid dance band for this evening. It's been years since anyone has brought in a regular professional band for a high school party. The kids will be talking about this for weeks. It will *make* you socially, Marilyn. It will just make you." With that she swept out of the room and was away to check the last minute details.

Marilyn went to the phone and tried to call Kay, but she had gone out early in the day to help one of the church ladies with her work. She almost called Danny, but with her hand on the phone she stopped. "That would be silly," she said to herself.

The afternoon dragged endlessly, but dinnertime came at last, and Marilyn had to get ready for the party. She went wearily upstairs and took her new formal off the hanger. All afternoon she had been praying. And for a while she felt as though everything was going to be all right. Now a thousand doubts seized her. Desperately she dropped to her knees and began to pray.

She was still on her knees when her mother rapped on her door. "Marilyn," she called sharply. "Marilyn! Are you about ready? We must be out at the country club in twenty minutes."

"I'll be there," Marilyn answered, getting to her feet and wiping away the tears.

She had not been out to the country club for months—ever since she had taken Christ as her Savior, in fact. She gasped when she did step inside and saw the beautiful ballroom. It was the most beautiful room!

"Do you like it?" Mrs. Forester beamed.

"Oh, it's beautiful, Mother."

"I decorated it all myself," her mother said.

It was a lovely setting, and as Marilyn stood inside the doorway greeting the well-dressed young people who came in, she found herself enjoying it.

Presently the band came out from one of the service entrances and began to play. A tall, blond lad approached her.

"May I have this dance, Marilyn?" he asked politely.

ELEVEN
The rescue

Marilyn stood on the edge of the dance floor in bewilderment and indecision. Several couples had already started to glide across the floor. Something about the music set the rhythm to tingling in her feet. For a brief instant she wanted to dance.

"May I have this dance, Marilyn?" the boy before her repeated.

Across the way her mother was scowling at her and motioning her toward the floor with a small, but unmistakable movement of her hand.

Marilyn took a half step toward him and stopped, tears flooding her eyes.

"What's the matter?" he asked softly. "What's wrong?"

"I just can't do it, Charles."

He took her by the arm and led her across one corner of the floor to an isolated spot at the far end of the long room. He was a tall, handsome boy who had graduated from high school the year before and was going to the university in Minneapolis.

"Now what's all this about?" he asked her gently when they were seated. "I only asked for the first dance."

"I know," she answered, her voice still trembling slightly. "And I'm sorry, Charles. It's just that I don't dance anymore and Mother insisted on having this party for me."

"You don't dance?" he repeated. "Would you mind telling me why? And why you are making such a fuss over it?"

"I'm a Christian now, Charles," she said. "I've given my heart to the Lord Jesus, and I feel it's better for me if I do not dance. But Mother has been insisting that I do."

He looked at her quizzically. "I don't get it, Marilyn," he said. "I mean, why should it make any difference whether you dance or not? What's that got to do with religion?"

She explained to him that the Bible gave very definite instructions about how a believer should live and what he should do. "Jesus tells us that we are to separate ourselves from the world," she said seriously. "And I feel that all this is a part of the world."

Charles Adams was obviously impressed. "But don't you think a person can be religious and dance?"

She was silent momentarily. "When I gave my heart to Christ, I gave him all. I know that even if I do the very best that I can, I'm going to fall far short of living the way I should. I've got to keep from doing the things that I'm convinced in my heart are wrong."

Mrs. Forester came mincing up just then. "Marilyn," she said, "don't you think you ought to dance and mingle with your guests?"

Charles got to his feet. "Marilyn and I are having a

fascinating conversation, Mrs. Forester," he said politely. "I hope you aren't going to take her away from me."

"Oh, not at all, Charles. Only I thought perhaps . . ." Her voice trailed away and she faded back into the shadows.

"Thank you, Charles," Marilyn told him when her mother had gone.

"If you've got convictions like that, I'm for you." He got to his feet. "Why don't you and I walk around among the kids and talk with them. If anyone asks you to dance, I'll tell them you are with me."

Marilyn smiled and took his arm. "You know," she said gratefully, "ever since Mother started to plan this party I've been praying about it. I knew that she was going to insist that I dance. I didn't want to disobey her, but I just couldn't think about getting out on the dance floor. God certainly works things out."

"You've got me interested in God," he told her seriously. "I'm going to look into it when I get back to school."

That night when the party was finally over Mrs. Forester came over to where Marilyn and Charles were standing.

"Well, my dear," she beamed, "how did you enjoy the party?"

"It was fine, Mother," she said.

"It was so much better than being with those religious friends of yours, wasn't it?"

"Marilyn seems to have a very sensible religion," Charles said. "It was the first time I've ever heard anything quite like it. I must confess that it has intrigued me."

Mrs. Forester turned to her daughter and lifted her eyebrows mockingly. "You mean you spent such a beautiful evening talking religion? You have it worse than I thought, my dear." With that she turned and swept away.

Marilyn rode home with her mother after the last guest had departed. Once or twice she tried to talk to her, but she drove in icy silence. They went into the house and took off their coats.

"Good night, Mother," the girl ventured timidly.

Mrs. Forester turned to stare at her. "I was never so humiliated in all my life," she choked.

The next morning was Sunday, and Danny got up at his usual time, dressed for Sunday school, and went downstairs.

Kirk came down wearing a pair of jeans and his pajama top. Mr. and Mrs. Meyer had left early to be gone for the day and had left Kirk home with Danny.

"Boy, you don't look much like going to Sunday school," Danny said, smiling.

"I don't think I'm going this morning," Kirk said, disinterestedly. "It's just the same old thing every Sunday. I'm going to stay at home and read these. I've got to give them back to a kid tomorrow."

Danny sat down at the table across from him. "Do you think you're doing what God wants you to do?" he asked. "Do you think it's better for you to stay at home from Sunday school to read comics, Kirk?"

The younger boy flushed. "You don't need to act like it's such a terrible sin, Danny," he retorted. "I'm just going to stay at home this one Sunday, that's all."

Tim had been going to Sunday school and church

regularly, but that Sunday morning he was not there. Danny wondered about it, and that afternoon he walked over to the little house where Tim and his mother lived.

Mrs. Barton scowled at him when she came to the door, but she called Tim who came quickly.

"Hi, Danny," he said pleasantly. "I was just going to come over and see you."

"You weren't in Sunday school this morning," Danny said, "and I thought maybe you were under the weather."

"Couldn't make it today," Tim said, getting his coat and heavy cap. "Let's go downtown and see what's going on." When they were away from the house he stopped. "I wanted to come to church this morning," he said, "but just as I got ready to leave, Dad came by."

"That's good," Danny said. He knew how much Tim had been worrying about his father even though he hadn't said anything about him for weeks.

"Mother wasn't home when he got there," Tim said, "and I had a chance to talk to him. I told him about the Lord and how I had taken Christ as my Savior."

"What did he say to that?"

"It was the strangest thing," he went on. "When I told Dad about how I had put my trust in Jesus Christ, he got the funniest look on his face. He told me then that his mother had been a Christian and had pleaded with him to take Christ as his Savior. But he determined to live his own life. And, he said to me, 'look what a mess I have made of it.'" Tim stopped a minute, the smile gone from his face. "I believe," he said, "that my Dad did accept Christ. He said he was tired of living his kind of life. If Mother had not come home when she did I–I might have been able to go deeper with Dad."

"We'll have to keep praying for him, Tim."

"I wonder whether that would get Mother and Dad together again," he said sadly. "She wouldn't look at him or talk to him today, and he had not been drinking. I do not think he's had anything to drink since he left."

"We don't want to forget," Danny said firmly, "that 'all things are possible with God.'"

That afternoon when Marilyn came home from church, Mrs. Forester was sitting primly in the living room, her hands folded in her lap.

"Marilyn, come over here and sit down."

"What's up, Mother?"

Mrs. Forester said no more until her daughter had taken a chair across from her.

"Marilyn," she began, "I was never so humiliated and upset in my life. To think that you would spend all of last evening at your party talking with Peggy Adams' boy about religion." She stopped and pursed her lips.

"I was just explaining to Charles about how I did not want to dance," Marilyn said, "and why."

"You had him so upset that he went over to that dumpy little church across the street from their place this morning," her mother snapped. "She called me a few minutes ago and was laughing so hard that she was almost hysterical. She said that you would make a preacher out of Charles yet."

"But all I did, Mother," Marilyn replied, "was to talk to Charles a—"

"I know what you did," her mother cut in. "I'll never be able to live this down. All the girls at the club will know. I'll be the laughingstock of our group. And to think, I worked for hours on this party. And you don't appreciate it any more than that."

"I–I'm sorry, Mother."

"That's not enough, Marilyn," Mrs. Forester retorted. "You've got to give up this foolishness. You've got to quit running around with those religious fanatics. You're going to have to start traveling with the group that attended your party last night."

"But I can't do that, Mother," Marilyn protested. "We don't have things in common. They do a lot of things that I can't do, and I do things that they don't do. It just wouldn't work at all."

"It's going to work one way or another," Mrs. Forester clipped. She straightened and unfolded her hands. "Marilyn," she said determinedly, "I have made up my mind. I'm going to send you to a private school. There you will learn to dance and learn the social graces. They'll set you straight on this religious fanaticism."

TWELVE
More than a miracle

When Danny and Tim finished their ice cream, they walked over to the place where Danny Orlis stayed.

They stepped over a pile of comic books on the third step of the stairway and went up to Danny's room. "What's this?" Danny exclaimed as he saw the note on the door. "Danny," he read. "Call Kay as soon as you get home. She says that it's very, very important. Kirk."

When Kay answered the phone she sounded as though she had been crying. "Marilyn is here," Kay said, "and something terrible has happened. We'd like to talk to you right away."

"Sure thing."

Tim called his mother and then the two boys hurried down to Kay's house where she and Marilyn were waiting.

"It isn't that I mind going to a private school," Marilyn explained, "even though it would be awfully hard; I'd hate to leave all you kids in the Bible club and Young People's. But it's not that. It's that they all dance—all the kids who go there. They play bridge and go to the theater and everything. I'm afraid to go. I don't know how my faith could stand it."

"God can keep you from those things," Kay told her.

"I know that. But if I have to spend a year there, I'm afraid I might get to liking them. I might not want to stand firm for the Lord."

"Couldn't we go and talk to your mother?"

"That would never do," Marilyn replied quickly.

"How about your dad?" Kay asked. "Would it do any good to talk to him about it? Perhaps you could make him understand why you don't want to go away to school."

"He's never paid any attention to things like that before. I don't think he'd say a word."

"It's like I told you when you worried about the dance, Marilyn," Kay put in. "We shouldn't do a thing ourselves until we've asked the Lord to work things out."

Marilyn Forester smiled. "I wish I had faith like yours. You make everything sound so simple."

"Prayer is the first thing," Danny said. "Too often we do everything we can and then we finally pray. That's just the opposite way we ought to do."

"I've got an idea," Kay said. "Let's decide that every night at ten o'clock, wherever we are or whatever we're doing, we'll stop and pray."

Despite the fact that Danny had spoken with a great deal of confidence to Marilyn, when he and Kay were alone a little later, doubts began to creep into his mind.

"I don't know about Marilyn," he said thoughtfully. "I'm afraid I don't have the faith to believe that very much can be done to help her."

"Maybe we could talk to her dad and get him to see

that Marilyn shouldn't go to the school her mother has chosen."

"Mrs. Meyer and I went and talked with Tim's mother," Danny said, "and almost got our heads chewed off."

"But we can try, can't we? I mean the worst he can do is to order us out."

"Well," Danny said resignedly. "If you're game, I guess I am."

Kay looked at her watch. "I think Mrs. Forester still goes to that Sunday evening bridge club," she said. "Why don't we go to church tonight and then walk over by Marilyn's and see if her dad is home?"

"OK," he replied. "Marilyn won't be there. She and Tim are going to church together."

They went to the services as they had planned. When it was over they walked through the cold night air to the Forester home. Marilyn's dad was just taking off his coat. They could see him standing in the front hall.

"I'm glad you came to see me tonight," he said. "I'm planning on taking the midnight train east on a buying trip and will be gone almost a month."

"We wanted to talk to you about Marilyn," Kay said hesitantly. "She doesn't want to go to that private school."

"Her mother and I have talked that over. It's the only thing to do. When a girl begins to get out of hand it's better to deal with it early."

"But, Mr. Forester," Kay said hesitantly, "the reason Marilyn doesn't want to go to that school is that she'll be expected to do things that she feels she shouldn't do as a Christian."

"Her mother says she's getting a warped personality," he went on. "It isn't good to have religion occupy her mind so much that she won't think of anything else."

"What about Mr. Meyer?" Danny asked him softly. "Do you think his personality has become warped since he took Christ as his Savior?"

There was a short silence.

"I'd never actually thought of that. One of the men at the office remarked only Friday that he'd noticed the change that's come over Meyer in the past few months."

"Both Marilyn and Mr. Meyer are trusting the same Lord," Kay put in. "Marilyn hasn't stayed out late at night or had poor grades or anything like that, has she?"

Mr. Forester got to his feet. "I'll tell you what I'll do," he said. "I'll think this over and talk to Meyer about it."

"But, Mr. Forester," Danny said, "if you don't do that tonight, Marilyn might be in that school by the time you get home. Then it will be too late."

Mr. Forester tightened his lips but said nothing.

When they were outside, Danny turned to Kay. "Well, what do you think?"

"Let's just keep praying about it."

The next morning when Danny went to school he looked for Marilyn in the hall, but she knew nothing more than she had before.

"Mother said she was going to go to Duluth with me next Saturday to get the clothes I'll need."

Danny started to tell her that he and Kay had gone to see her dad the night before, but changed his mind.

98

"Just keep trusting," he told her instead.

When he got into his division room, his classmates crowded around him excitedly. "Did you see the paper this morning?" they asked.

"Didn't get up in time," he answered.

"Look," one of them exclaimed, opening the Minneapolis paper to the sports page. "Let me read this. 'Two of the finest high school backs in the country have just played their last games for Cedarton in Northern Minnesota. Tim Barton, last year's All-State quarterback from Duluth, and Danny Orlis sparked the powerful Cedarton eleven to an undefeated season. The university that lands that combination is going to be grabbing off the hottest football prospects this reporter has ever seen!'"

Danny felt the color come up into his cheeks and he smiled somewhat self-consciously. There was no denying that it made him feel good to hear things like that.

"Man, oh, man," one of the boys said, taking the paper to read the account again. "Just think of that! Have any of the big schools approached you yet? What kind of a deal can you get, Danny?"

"I had a guy talk to me a little," the Orlis boy admitted. "But he asked me not to tell who he was. And he didn't make a regular offer. He just said that he'd like to talk to me before I made up my mind."

Coach Collins came up then. He, too, was carrying a copy of the morning *Tribune*. "I see that you've seen the paper, Danny," he said. "I'd like to talk to you for a couple of minutes."

"Sure thing," Danny answered. The two of them went down the hall to the coach's office.

"I couldn't help hearing that you'd been approached

by a university about playing for them," Collins said when they were in his office. "You've played for me this year and did a lot to make this season a success, and I'd like to help you in the selection of a school, if I may. At least I'd like to talk with you about it sometime."

"Sure," Danny told him. "I don't have the slightest idea where I should go."

"I think I can help you to get a good deal with a good top school," Coach Collins went on. "When you do get ready to decide, why don't you come and talk with me before you definitely make up your mind."

"I'll do that," Danny promised.

That evening at the dinner table Marilyn sat across from her mother. Her eyes were red and swollen and she ate very little.

"Now you might just as well quit that sniveling," Mrs. Forester told her. "When you get to Brownwell Hall you'll get in with some lovely girls and have a wonderful time."

Marilyn said nothing.

"I'm going to buy you some beautiful dresses, my dear," her mother went on, "and some dancing slippers, and if you'll stop this crying, I'll talk Daddy into getting you a fur stole."

"I know you're trying to help me, Mother," Marilyn replied, "and I do appreciate it, but I don't want those things. What I want more than anything else in the world is to live the way that Christ wants me to live."

Mrs. Forester bit her trembling lip.

They heard the front door open.

"Who's that, Mother?"

An instant later her dad walked into the kitchen, his suitcase in his hand.

"Harold!" Mrs. Forester exclaimed. "What are you doing home? I thought you were going to be gone a month."

"So did I." He set his suitcase down and kissed them. "But I had a change of plans."

"You have not eaten, Harold," his wife said, getting up and going over to the cabinet. "I'll get you a plate."

"What happened, Daddy?"

"It's quite a long story," he said, sitting down beside her. "I went to see John Meyer last night before I left for the train. He gave me a book to read. On the way down to Minneapolis, I read most of the night. And when I got there, I decided that I had to come back."

"What do you mean?" Mrs. Forester asked him.

"You see," Mr. Forester went on slowly, "he talked with me about my soul. And when I left he gave me his New Testament to read." He paused and took a deep breath. "I accepted the Lord Jesus as my Savior on the train last night!"

A radiant smile broke across Marilyn's face. Mrs. Forester's face evidenced her displeasure. She clasped each side of the table with trembling hands.

"It isn't true, Harold!" she gasped at last. "No, it can't be!"

THIRTEEN
A new dawn

For the space of a minute, Mrs. Forester sat motionless, staring across the table at her husband.

"You can't mean it, Harold. You're joking."

"No, Carrie," he spoke softly, "I've never been more serious in my life."

There was a long silence. "First, my daughter." Her voice sounded dull and far away. "Now, my husband. It could be funny if it weren't so—so tragic."

"It isn't tragic," Harold said, smiling. "It's wonderful. It's the most wonderful thing that ever happened to me."

Mrs. Forester swallowed hard and became very nervous.

"We've had almost everything we've wanted, you and I. We have a fine home, a nice car, and a large enough income to belong to the better clubs and associate with anyone in Cedarton. But it's been an empty thing, Carrie. You know we haven't been happy, not *really* happy. And neither have most of our friends."

He reached out and clasped his wife's hand in his own. It was damp with perspiration, and trembling.

She started to speak, then stopped.

"Last night," he told her, "as I read the Bible and thought about what Meyer told me, I began to see that he and Marilyn have something that we do not have. Their lives have purpose and direction. And now that I've taken Christ as my Savior, I have that same purpose and direction."

"Don't!" Mrs. Forester broke in quickly. Tears flooded her eyes. "I can't stand it, Harold!" With that she pushed noisily back from the table and got to her feet. She started to speak, then choked suddenly and burst into tears.

"Now, Carrie."

She turned and fled upstairs.

Mariyln and her father stood there, staring at one another uneasily. Harold Forester shook his head sorrowfully. Marilyn started to cry.

"Oh, Daddy, Daddy, I'm so happy for you, but—" she stopped and wiped away the tears.

"If only your mother and I could have seen our need of a Savior when we were first married," he said at last. "We didn't have much money or position or anything else to stand in the way." He was silent for a moment. "Perhaps things could have been different."

A tear that had been clinging, full and luminous, to Marilyn's long eyelashes lost its hold and trickled down her cheek.

"I'd be so happy if Mother would only accept Christ as her Savior," she choked. "But it's going to be so wonderful to have a Christian daddy."

"I pray that God will help me to be the kind of a father I should be."

The clock in the living room struck seven times. She waited until the last chime died away.

"You'll never know how hard I've been praying for you both, Daddy," she said, "You accepted Christ with just me praying for you. With both of us praying, I know that Mother will take Jesus as her Savior soon."

"I certainly hope so." He started up the stairs, stopped, and turned back. "And Marilyn," he continued, "don't worry about that private school business. I can understand now why you don't want to go. Just forget it and leave it to me."

She threw her arms about his neck and kissed him.

When her father finally went upstairs, Marilyn rushed to the telephone to call Kay.

"I've got something to tell you," she said excitedly. "Could I meet you and Danny right away?"

"Why don't you come here? I'll call Danny."

Marilyn stood with the telephone in her hand a moment or two after her friend had hung up. It scarcely seemed real. It had all happened so quickly she could hardly believe that her father had actually taken the Lord Jesus as his personal Savior. But it was true. There was his suitcase in the hall. There was his coat thrown over the back of the chair. She listened an instant at the stairs. She could hear her parents talking.

"I'm going down to meet a couple of kids," she called up to them. "I'll be back in about an hour."

Kay and Danny were waiting for her when she arrived.

"What's the trouble?" Kay said excitedly.

"It's so wonderful I can hardly talk," Marilyn began breathlessly. "Daddy just accepted Christ as his Savior, and I don't have to go to that private school. Things will be so different." Marilyn took a deep breath and paused a moment.

"Oh, I'm so happy for you!" Kay exclaimed.

The next morning when Marilyn got up and came down for breakfast her father was sitting in the kitchen with the New Testament Mr. Meyer had given him. He looked up.

"Why don't you read it aloud, Daddy?" she asked, sitting across the table from him.

"All right," he replied. He started at the beginning of the chapter and read aloud. Marilyn sat listening. When he had finished they both bowed their heads and prayed together.

"This is nice, Marilyn," her dad said as they raised their heads. "Why don't we do this every morning?"

She smiled happily. "It's the happiest, most wonderful morning of my life!"

"If only Mother would see her need."

"She will, Daddy," Marilyn said confidently. "We'll pray and pray and pray until she does."

THE DANNY ORLIS ADVENTURE SERIES

DON'T MISS ALL SIX EXCITING BOOKS ABOUT DANNY ORLIS AND HIS ADVENTURES!

The Final Touchdown
The Last Minute Miracle
The Race Against Time
The Showdown
The Case of the Talking Rocks
The Sacred Ruins

The Danny Orlis adventure series is available at your local bookstore, or you may order by mail (U.S. and territories only). Send your check or money order for $2.95 plus $.75 for postage and handling per book ordered to:

Tyndale D.M.S.
P.O. Box 80
Wheaton, IL 60189

Prices subject to change. Allow 4–6 weeks for delivery.

Tyndale House Publishers, Inc.
Wheaton, Illinois